I AM AN AMERICAN

I AM AN AMERICAN

A True Story
of Japanese Internment

by Jerry Stanley

CROWN PUBLISHERS, INC., NEW YORK

Previous page: *Families, including children wearing registration tags, leave by truck from Redondo Beach, California, for a relocation center.*

Published by Crown Publishers, Inc., a Random House company, 201 East 50th Street, New York, New York 10022

CROWN is a trademark of Crown Publishers, Inc.

Manufactured in the United States of America

Maps copyright © 1994 by Magellan Geographix[SM] Santa Barbara, California

Library of Congress Cataloging-in-Publication Data
Stanley, Jerry, 1941–
I am an American : a true story of Japanese internment / by Jerry Stanley.
p. cm.
Includes bibliographical references and index.
1. Japanese Americans—Evacuation and relocation, 1942–1945—Juvenile literature. 2. World War, 1939–1945—Concentration Camps—United States—Juvenile literature. 3. World War, 1939–1945—United States—Juvenile literature. 4. United States—Ethnic relations—Juvenile literature. [1. Japanese Americans—Evacuation and relocation. 2. World War, 1939–1945—United States.]
I. Title.
D769.8.A6S73   1994
940.53' 1503956073—dc20   93-41330

ISBN 0-517-59786-1 (trade)
0-517-59787-X (lib. bdg.)

10 9 8 7 6 5 4 3 2 1

First Edition

Picture credits appear on page 97.

CONTENTS

PRONUNCIATION

*

Issei pronounced EES-say

Nisei pronounced KNEE-say

Introduction: A DATE WHICH WILL LIVE IN INFAMY

On December 7, 1941, Japanese warplanes bombed the United States Naval Base at Pearl Harbor, Hawaii. The surprise attack destroyed nineteen ships, killed 2,335 servicemen, and led the United States to declare war on Japan and her allies, Germany and Italy. Shocked at the destruction of the Seventh Fleet and the loss of American lives, President Franklin D. Roosevelt proclaimed December 7, 1941, "a date which will live in infamy."

December 7, 1941: Explosions during the Japanese attack on Pearl Harbor.

The bombing of Pearl Harbor was a great tragedy in American history, but it resulted in a second tragedy that was no less important: the forced imprisonment in the United States of 120,000 people, two-thirds of whom were United States citizens. These citizens had committed no crime, broken no law, and when their rights were taken away, they were charged with no offense. Their only crime was that they were of Japanese ancestry.

The Japanese imprisoned during World War II belonged to one of two groups, called Issei and Nisei. The Issei were Japanese citizens who had immigrated to America to better their lives. But unlike immigrants from England, France, and other European countries, the Issei could not become citizens of the United States. The Naturalization Act of 1790 limited citizenship to "any alien, being a free white person." Although African Americans had been granted citizenship in 1870, Asians were considered nonwhite.

The children of the Issei were known as Nisei. Because they were born in America, they were automatically citizens of the United States. They had the same rights as any citizen, and they were proud to be Americans.

America was the only country the Nisei knew, and so they spoke English, not Japanese, and practiced American customs. The Issei liked rice and raw fish; the Nisei liked hamburgers and malts. The Issei were Buddhists; the Nisei were Christians. The Issei liked to play Go, a Japanese game similar to checkers; the Nisei liked to play baseball and football and dance to the big bands of the day.

Unlike their parents, the Nisei acted and thought of themselves as Americans. To gain acceptance as Americans, in 1930 the Nisei formed the Japanese American Citizens League,

which was influential in Washington, Oregon, and California, the area where 95 percent of the Japanese lived. Its purpose was to fight discrimination against the Japanese and demonstrate Nisei loyalty to America. Members displayed pride in their American citizenship by reciting a pledge:

I am proud that I am an American citizen of Japanese ancestry, for my very background makes me appreciate more fully the wonderful advantages of this nation. I believe in her institutions, ideals, and her future. I am firm

Nisei high school students in San Francisco in 1942. Young Japanese Americans shared the clothes and customs of their white American contemporaries.

in my belief that American sportsmanship and attitude of fair play will judge citizenship and patriotism on the basis of action and achievement and not on the basis of physical characteristics.

But despite their loyalty, on February 19, 1942, President Roosevelt authorized the removal of all Japanese from the west coast and their confinement in relocation camps—not because they had done anything wrong but only because they were Japanese. The detention of these American citizens was known as Japanese internment, and the following story is about the experiences of one of those citizens, Shiro Nomura, who was a senior in high school when he was forced to leave home and live behind a barbed wire fence. An American citizen by birth—as well as by choice—Shiro had never been to Japan. He did not read, speak, or understand Japanese, and he was fiercely loyal to America. At the time of the bombing of Pearl Harbor, he was in love with a girl named Amy and was about to propose marriage when his plans were shattered by race prejudice and war. For him, and the other citizens imprisoned during World War II, February 19, 1942, was also a date "which will live in infamy."

1 . THE GATHERING STORM

SHIRO'S PARENTS, HACHIZO AND TSURU NOMURA, were Issei and their experiences were typical of Japanese who immigrated to America. They grew up together in Fukuoka, Japan, married at an early age, and in 1900 immigrated to Hawaii, where laborers were needed for chopping sugarcane and harvesting pineapple. Because Hachizo could say "yes" and "no" in English, he soon became a crew chief. He saved the extra money he earned, and in 1905 used it to relocate in Berkeley, California. Hachizo leased farmland and grew fruits and vegetables. Like other Issei farmers in northern California, he shipped his produce to local markets, providing city dwellers with fresh food at low prices.

Shiro's parents arrived in California just before the San Francisco School Board Crisis of 1906, which set off an anti-Japanese movement that would last for twenty years. In 1900 there were nearly 25,000 Japanese in the United States. By 1910 their population had reached nearly 70,000, most of them farmers or laborers in California. Like the Nomuras, they were truck farmers. They were not in competition with most white farmers, who shipped their crops to eastern markets. But by working long hours and carefully cultivating the soil, the Issei made their farmland the richest in California.

Many Issei took land that whites had given up on, and they made it produce fruits, vegetables, berries, and even grapes. Others, such as George Shima, drained swampland and made it profitable. In the Sacramento Valley, Shima created a potato

Hachizo and Tsuru Nomura.

farming empire that employed 500 people and won him the nickname the Potato King. Among the new crops the Japanese introduced in California were strawberries, blackberries, raspberries, and cauliflower.

Japanese farmers in Los Angeles, 1893.

Whites began to complain that they could not compete against the Japanese farmers, and labor unions began to agitate against cheap Japanese workers. These same arguments had already been used against the Chinese, with the result that Chinese immigration was prohibited in 1882. In 1906 the *San Francisco*

Chronicle began calling for an end to all Japanese immigration. Building on hostility toward the Chinese, the *Chronicle* headlined

BROWN ARTISANS STEAL BRAINS OF WHITES

THE YELLOW PERIL—HOW JAPANESE CROWD OUT THE WHITE RACE

While the *Chronicle* issued these warnings, labor unions in San Francisco formed the Asiatic Exclusion League and the Anti-Jap Laundry League to campaign for an end to Japanese immigration. At street-corner rallies, they fired up crowds with the slogan that would be repeated after the bombing of Pearl Harbor: The Japs Must Go! Japanese restaurants were boycotted, Japanese trucks were overturned, and rotten eggs were thrown at Japanese laundries.

Responding to public sentiment, the San Francisco Board of Education voted in October 1906 to segregate its schools on the basis of race. It ordered the ninety-three Japanese students in the district to a segregated school in Chinatown. Twenty-five of the students were Nisei, citizens of the United States.

The board's action triggered a diplomatic crisis between the United States and Japan. Japan demanded that the United States obey the 1894 treaty between the two countries, which granted equal rights to citizens of both countries. The crisis was resolved when President Theodore Roosevelt persuaded the board to cancel its segregation order. In return, Roosevelt got Japan to consent to a "gentlemen's agreement" by which Japan voluntarily stopped the immigration of Japanese men to the United States. However, Japanese women, called picture brides, continued to immigrate to America in order to marry Issei men, further angering white Californians. In 1920 California would succeed in

A Japanese farm family, Montebello, California, 1914.

getting a "ladies' agreement" that stopped the immigration of Japanese women.

California created another diplomatic crisis when it passed the Alien Land Law of 1913. This legislation banned further purchases of land by Issei and limited their leases on farmland to three years. Most families (including the Nomuras) got around this law by transferring land titles to their Nisei offspring, who had the right to own property because they were American citizens. Thereafter, California concentrated on prohibiting further Japanese immigration. The state finally succeeded in getting Congress to pass the Immigration Act of 1924, which halted all Japanese immigration to America.

Nevertheless, the Japanese continued to farm successfully in California. In 1920 they owned or leased only 4 percent of

California's improved cropland, but sales of Issei fruits and vegetables accounted for 11 percent of the total value of the state's truck crops. By 1940 the average value per acre for all farms in Washington, Oregon, and California was $37.94; for Japanese farms it was $279.96. After the bombing of Pearl Harbor, white farmers again wanted Issei land. "We are charged with wanting to get rid of the Japs for selfish reasons," said a spokesman for the white farmers in 1942. "We do. If all the Japs were removed tomorrow, we'd never miss them because the white farmers can take over and produce everything the Jap grows. And we don't want them back either."

In spite of the anti-Japanese movement, by the early 1920s Hachizo and Tsuru Nomura had become successful farmers in Berkeley and had established a family. Shigeru Nomura was born in 1914 and his sister Sadae in 1917. But bad luck hit the family in September 1923 when a massive fire destroyed most of Berkeley. Along with other Issei, the family's livelihood was wiped out. The

Strawberry beds in front of a farmhouse in California in 1942. This farm was home to a family of ten—eight children born in the United States and their Japanese-born parents.

blaze destroyed Hachizo's truck, the family home, and many of their possessions.

Hoping for a better life in another part of California, Hachizo and Tsuru decided to move to southern California and try farming once again. As the family was preparing to leave Berkeley, Shiro was born.

The move to southern California was fortunate, for Shiro's childhood could not have been more different from his parents' experiences in northern California. Southern California in the 1930s was largely rural, and farming was open to anyone who was willing to work hard and contribute to the area's economy. Here the Japanese established thriving communities, and their Nisei children blended into white society.

The Nomura family settled in Keystone, ten miles southwest of the growing city of Los Angeles. Hachizo bought forty acres of land in his oldest son's name; planted carrots, celery, lettuce, and tomatoes; and trucked his crops to an open-air market in Long Beach. Many of Hachizo's relatives had already moved to southern California, and their Nisei children helped work the Nomuras' farm as Shiro reached his teens.

As a student at Banning High School, Shiro adopted the nickname Shi (pronounced SHY). He was one of only eighteen Nisei, so most of his friends were white. A keen athlete whose world was dominated by sports, Shi was a starting pitcher in baseball, a wide receiver in football, and co-captain of the varsity track team, where he excelled in hurdles and the shot put. But something else made him popular at Banning High. As his friend Keith Tatsuno explained: "Shi was one of the best-looking guys in the school."

"I was a girl chaser," Shi recalled. "I thought mostly about

EVELYN HARNER
LEONARD HUASTES

JACK HURLEY
ANNETTE KERNS

EUNICE KOOKEN
MASAO IWAMOTO

CHARLES LAPSLEY
LEONA LUTHER

DORIS MESSENGER
ARTHUR McKENZIE

GLENN MORRISON
DORIS MOORE

RUTH MORITA
SHIRO NOMURA

BEN OKURA
ANNA BELLE MUNN

A page from Shi Nomura's high school yearbook. Shi is pictured on the right in the second row from the bottom.

girls and sports." At the school's Friday night dances Shi and his friends danced to the hit records of the Glenn Miller, Tommy Dorsey, and Benny Goodman bands. Afterward, the boys and their girlfriends went to a local hangout called Sally's for hamburgers, malts, and hot apple pie. In 1940 Shi met Emiko Hattori, who as a young girl had changed her name to Amy.

Amy Hattori, 1941.

Like the Nomuras, Amy's family had lived in California for nearly forty years. Her father had a graduate degree from a Japanese university, but when he arrived in San Francisco he found few jobs open to Asians. He worked as a houseboy and married Tora Hayashica, who came to California as a picture bride before the ladies' agreement of 1920. In the 1920s the Hattori family moved to Los Angeles, where Amy's father opened a produce market. While a student at Roosevelt High School, Amy and her younger sister Susie helped to manage the Toyo Hotel in the Japanese section of town. Recalling her teenage years when she dated Nisei and non-Nisei boys, Amy said, "Most of my friends were white and I never felt set off."

Amy was a sophomore and Shi had just started his junior year when they met on a blind date. They were soon in love, and Shi planned to propose marriage upon graduation. But at a track meet in his senior year Shi was struck in the head by a shot put. The accident left him paralyzed for six months and forced him to postpone any thought of marriage.

Another event around this time left a deep impression on Shi. In August 1941 Shi took Amy to the annual Nisei Week Festival, a celebration of Japanese culture held at Yamato Hall in Los Angeles. During the evening Shi was held spellbound by a teenage girl singing a song called "Liebestraum" in a strong, beautiful voice. With Amy at his side, he did no more than listen. But he never forgot the girl at Yamato Hall.

Then Shi's world was shattered by history. Four months after he attended the festival at Yamato Hall, Japan bombed Pearl Harbor, ending Shi's hope of finishing high school, marrying Amy, or perhaps meeting the girl at Yamato Hall.

2. EXECUTIVE ORDER NO. 9066

ON THE NIGHT OF DECEMBER 6, 1941, after taking Amy home from a date, Shi's car was hit from behind. Shi suffered numerous cuts to his face. When his father saw him the next day, Hachizo thought his son had been attacked by a gang of whites in retaliation for the bombing of Pearl Harbor that morning.

"We were unaware at the time," Shi recalled, "but December 7, 1941, was the beginning of a series of events that were nightmarish and almost unbelievable. During the days following Pearl Harbor, many friendships withered while others were severely tested. The usual places of recreation became uncomfortable. It was the start of a very painful period."

After Pearl Harbor the Nisei went to great lengths to demonstrate their patriotism. They flooded the streets of San Francisco, Los Angeles, and Seattle in mass demonstrations of loyalty. They waved American flags and recited the pledge of the Japanese American Citizens League. They bought war bonds, donated blood, and ran ads in newspapers denouncing Japan and pledging loyalty to America. In San Francisco, Nisei started a fund-raising campaign to buy bombs for attacking Tokyo. In Los Angeles they formed committees to make sure that no person of Japanese ancestry tried to aid Japan. The day after Pearl Harbor

Above and opposite: Children at the Raphael Weill Public School in San Francisco recite the Pledge of Allegiance during a flag ceremony in the spring of 1942. The Japanese American children were moved to relocation camps soon after these pictures were taken.

the Japanese American Citizens League sent the following telegram to President Roosevelt:

> In this solemn hour we pledge our fullest cooperation to you, Mr. President, and to our country. There can not be any question. . . . We in our hearts know we are Americans, loyal to America.

At first, the demonstrations of loyalty brought pledges of support from government officials, and Japanese internment seemed unlikely. California Congressman Leland Ford said, "These people are American-born. This is their country." United

States Attorney General Francis Biddle declared, "At no time will the government engage in wholesale condemnation of any alien group."

The only action Biddle took in December was to move against enemy aliens—that is, German, Italian, and Japanese citizens living in the United States. He ordered the Federal Bureau of Investigation to arrest approximately 16,000 enemy aliens suspected of espionage or sabotage, but within weeks he released two-thirds of them. At the same time, the FBI and the Federal Communications Commission conducted separate investigations

of the Japanese living in America. Both investigations concluded that the Nisei were loyal citizens and that their Issei parents had taken no action to aid Japan.

It was a series of Japanese victories in the Pacific that started the movement to intern the Japanese. Japan captured Guam on December 13, 1941, Hong Kong on December 24, Manila on January 2, 1942, and Singapore on February 15.

Alarmed at the enemy's swift advance through the Pacific, military officials suggested that Japan might try to invade the west coast of America and that maybe the Issei and Nisei who lived there would aid the invasion. The Western Defense Commander, Lieutenant General John L. DeWitt, who was responsible for the security of the Pacific coast, was influential in spreading the idea that the Japanese might be disloyal. Following the loss of Manila he said, "I have little confidence that the Japanese enemy aliens [Issei] are loyal. I have no confidence in the loyalty of the Nisei whatsoever."

DeWitt's distrust appeared to be confirmed in the Roberts Report, a government investigation of the bombing of Pearl Harbor. Issued at about the time Singapore fell to Japan in February, the report blamed the disaster on lack of military preparedness and on Japanese sabotage in Hawaii. It even suggested that Japanese farmers had planted their crops in the shape of arrows pointing to Pearl Harbor as the target.

Although the charge of Japanese sabotage on Hawaii was totally false, newspaper writers and radio broadcasters began warning of the danger of Japanese sabotage on the west coast. In Los Angeles, radio commentator John Hughes warned that "Ninety percent or more of American-born Japanese are primarily loyal to Japan." In San Francisco, columnist Henry McLemore

Lieutenant General John L. DeWitt.

wrote, "I am for immediate removal of every Japanese on the West Coast. . . . Herd 'em up, pack 'em off. Let 'em be pinched, hurt and hungry!" Reflecting a tendency to confuse the enemy nation of Japan with American citizens of Japanese ancestry, McLemore thundered, "I hate the Japanese. And that goes for all of them!"

By late January 1942 rumors of Japanese sabotage were circulating on the west coast. It was reported that Japanese in the hills near Seattle had ignited a "flaming arrow" pointing toward the city to guide bombers to that target. The "flaming arrow" was brush being burned by forest workers. It was reported that Japanese farmers had covered their tomato plants with white cloth to form an arrow showing the way to a southern California aircraft plant. The tomatoes were capped with paper to protect against frost and were planted in a field that happened to come to a point. Rumor had it that Nisei fishermen in Los Angeles had Japanese naval uniforms hidden in their boats, just waiting for the invasion.

Japanese students at the University of California were suspected of subversion because some of them were enrolled in German-language classes. Why were they studying German, it was asked, if not to aid America's enemy? Of a total Japanese student population of 200, twenty-one were enrolled in German-language classes—along with 508 white students; a foreign language was required for graduation. In January 1942, after the FBI and the Federal Communications Commission had investigated the Japanese and found no evidence of disloyalty, General DeWitt and the newspaper writers made a crazy twist of logic. The fact that no evidence of sabotage had been found, they said, was proof that the Japanese *were* saboteurs. In other words,

Above: As hostility toward the Japanese increased, a Japanese American store owner displayed a sign in his store window proclaiming "I Am an American." Other business owners used their ancestry to differentiate themselves from the Japanese—such as this vegetable stand owner (**opposite**) who advertised his Filipino heritage.

the Japanese *must* be plotting sabotage because they had carefully covered up all evidence of it!

Meanwhile, newspapers incited the public by using the racial slur "Japs" when referring to both enemy soldiers and the Nisei. *Time* magazine carried the story "How to Tell Your Friends from the Japs." *Look* magazine carried the story "How to Tell Japs from the Chinese." Blurring the distinction between citizens of Japan and citizens of America, the *Los Angeles Times* insisted that Nisei were still "Japs": "A viper is a viper wherever the egg is hatched," the *Times* bellowed, "so a Japanese-American, born of Japanese parents, grows up to be Japanese, not an American."

With every passing day the hostility increased. Nisei tried to

join the army to defend their country but were turned away, declared ineligible because of their ancestry. In Seattle, Asians wore buttons reading "I Am a Chinese American" to distinguish themselves from the Japanese. In Los Angeles storefront windows displayed signs reading "No Japs." One Nisei in southern California recalled that "cars of Caucasian kids drove around the Japanese section yelling names at us, and we didn't have any comeback. There was always a fear of mob action." In the two months following Pearl Harbor there were thirty-six cases of gangs attacking the Japanese in the west coast states, resulting in the death of seven Nisei.

Stunned by the growing hostility, the Nisei tried to appear as un-Japanese as possible. Slowly, sadly, all along the west coast of America, they destroyed what they possessed of their Asian heritage. Japanese books and magazines were burned because of a rumor that FBI agents had found such materials in the homes of Issei arrested on suspicion of sabotage. Priceless diaries, letters, and photographs were burned; porcelain vases, tea sets, and silk tablecloths were buried or dumped on the street.

Mary Kageyama helped her older sister build a bonfire in the backyard to destroy their mother's sheet music, throwing stack after stack of Japanese operas on fine rice paper into the blaze. "We did it," Mary recalled, "because they wouldn't know what it said. They might think it was a code or something."

Frank Chuman was a student at the University of Southern California when he and his sister Yemi helped their parents burn Japanese-style clothing. But he recalled most vividly what his father did on the day of the burning.

My father went to a dresser in his bedroom where he kept two samurai swords, one long for two hands, the other short. These were family treasures, which had been handed down to him. His ancestors had been samurai, warriors of the Satsuma clan. I had looked forward to owning these swords some day, and many times had secretly taken them out to admire the magnificent blades. My father removed the swords from the beautiful inlaid cases, and he and I took them out into the backyard.

There he thrust both blades, bare and glistening, deep into the ground and we buried them. I was sad and it made me cry.

While the Japanese were destroying their possessions, General DeWitt moved to evacuate them from specific locations on the west coast. In late January 1942, Terminal Island in southern California was designated a "strategic area," prohibited to Japanese because it was near a naval base. FBI agents combed the island and removed the 500 Japanese families who lived there. Then, on January 29, DeWitt barred the Japanese from living near the San Francisco waterfront and the Los Angeles airport, declaring them strategic areas. Within the next ten days the Japanese were forced to vacate 133 areas around airports, power plants, and other places where, it was feared, sabotage *might* occur.

By mid-February the entire coastline of California was designated Restricted Area Number One. DeWitt issued a stern suggestion that the Japanese living in this coastal strip should voluntarily migrate inland. But when some 4,000 tried to move, they were met with hostility. Armed men patrolled the Nevada border to turn them back while main streets in Utah sported signs reading "No Japs Wanted." Because most people in the inland states had never met a person of Japanese ancestry, they decided that if the Japanese were a threat to California then they were also a threat to them.

After the voluntary evacuation plan failed, General DeWitt reversed himself and prohibited all Japanese from leaving Restricted Area Number One. First he said they should leave; now he ordered them to stay. And the Japanese turned back from

Restricted Area Number One

WASHINGTON

OREGON

Area of Detail

CALIFORNIA

*United States
Army personnel
work on evacuation
plans for Redondo
Beach, California,
in the spring of
1942.*

the interior were ordered to move back into the restricted area.
During this period one of DeWitt's staff described the general as
having "gone crazy."

Although they had defended the Japanese as loyal Americans
in December 1941, two months later the senators and
congressmen from California were calling for their removal.
Known as the California Hotheads, they convinced the
representatives from Washington and Oregon to support a
resolution for evacuation. To strengthen their argument, they
quoted California's Attorney General Earl Warren, who later
became chief justice of the United States Supreme Court. Warren
insisted, "There is more potential danger among the Japanese
who are born in this country than from the alien Japanese who

were born in Japan." Amazingly, Warren repeated General DeWitt's claim that the proof for Japanese American sabotage was the fact that none had been discovered.

Influenced by the rising tide of war hysteria and hate, on February 13, 1942, General DeWitt recommended the removal of all Japanese from the west coast. Believing the false rumors of sabotage, he justified removal on the grounds of "military necessity," although there has never been one proven example of Issei or Nisei disloyalty.

More important, America was also at war with Germany and Italy—but few citizens of German or Italian ancestry were interned during World War II. There were 51,923 Italian aliens and 19,422 German aliens living in California—more than all the Japanese aliens living in the United States. But only a handful of them were interned. In fact, on October 12, 1942, Attorney General Biddle announced that the 600,000 German citizens living in America were no longer considered "enemy aliens."

Like DeWitt, too many Americans made a distinction between people of Japanese ancestry and people of European ancestry. Only this explains why the Japanese were interned—but not white Europeans. Prejudice against the Japanese, building in California since 1906, was based on the idea that race, not citizenship, determined loyalty to America. "A Jap's a Jap," DeWitt thundered, "and it makes no difference if he is an American citizen."

Most Americans had never seen a Japanese and had never known one as a friend. This as much as anything else explains why they went along with the decision to remove the Japanese. A poll conducted in March 1942 found that 93 percent of Americans supported the evacuation of alien Japanese, and 59 percent

This Nisei soldier volunteered for the U.S. Army in 1941. In May 1942, he was granted leave to help his mother and family prepare for evacuation from their strawberry farm in Sacramento County, California, to a relocation camp. Many Japanese American soldiers saw their families imprisoned by the government they had volunteered to serve.

supported the removal of Japanese Americans who were citizens. One of the best examples of American citizens from different cultures not knowing one another occurred in March 1942, when a congressional committee traveled to the west coast to investigate the loyalty of the Japanese. Mike Masaoka was the first Nisei to appear before the committee. The congressmen were surprised that he spoke English so well, and they were surprised again when Mike said he could not read, write, or speak Japanese. They asked if he had ever attended a Japanese-language school where Nisei learned loyalty to the emperor of Japan. Mike said he had never attended a Japanese-language school—and had no desire to. They asked him if he had learned to worship the emperor on his trips to Japan. Mike answered that he had never been there (as was the case with 73 percent of the Nisei). They asked if he had learned emperor-worship by practicing Buddhism or Shinto. Mike said he was Mormon and the rest of his family were Presbyterians.

With no personal knowledge of the Japanese living in America, President Franklin D. Roosevelt yielded to pressure from the California Hotheads, the media, and the military. On February 19, 1942, Roosevelt signed Executive Order No. 9066, which gave the military the authority to remove enemy aliens and anyone else suspected of disloyalty. Although the document never mentioned the Japanese by name, it was understood that the order was meant for them alone. DeWitt was told he should act only against specific Germans and Italians whom he considered security risks. On March 2, DeWitt announced that all Japanese, regardless of citizenship, would be evacuated from Restricted Area Number One, the entire west coast, and placed in relocation camps. His racial argument had finally triumphed— "The Japanese race is an enemy race."

When authorities ordered the removal of the Japanese, Hideo Murata, an Issei veteran of the United States Army in World War I, thought the order was a practical joke. Hideo asked his friend, a sheriff, if he had heard right. Was this some funny mistake? It was no joke, the sheriff told him, and he would have to go to a camp. Instead, Hideo rented a hotel room and killed himself. When the sheriff found his lifeless body, he discovered, clutched in Hideo's hand, a certificate of honorary citizenship from Monterey County expressing "heartfelt gratitude, honor and respect for your loyal and splendid service to the country."

3 . E-Day

AMID THE GROWING HATRED AND VIOLENCE following Pearl Harbor, Shi's closest white friends stuck by him; it was not easy to do. Whites who defended the Nisei, or who were seen with them in public, were often suspected of disloyalty. The owner of a barber shop in Los Angeles refused to do business with other whites suspected of buying pastries from a Japanese store. In Tulare County, in central California, Joe Komori recalled, "One man who I thought was a friend told me, 'I don't like Japs or anyone who likes Japs.' He insulted my parents and wouldn't talk to us anymore."

The Japanese were refused admittance to movie theaters, cafés, and roller-skating rinks, while public parks displayed signs reading "No Japs." Hotels and restaurants fired their Japanese chefs, railroads discharged Issei foremen with perfect work records of thirty years, and some municipalities canceled Japanese-held licenses to operate grocery stores and cleaning shops. Shi remembered white mobs in southern California shouting, "Jap, go home!"

Battling the prejudice of the day was Shi's close friend and friend to the Nomura family, Ruby McFarland. "Handsome, grand, and genuine," Shi recalled, "Mrs. McFarland couldn't take the injustice being done to us. She went from one Japanese family to another, helping them and offering comfort. I wish more was said of the wonderful people like her who went to the aid of their Japanese friends."

The threat of violence and the awkward stares they received in public caused Shi and Amy to see less of one another in the early months of 1942. Separated by forty miles without the benefit of freeways, they stayed in their own neighborhoods and mostly indoors, fearful of the future. Those of Japanese ancestry could do little to protest the movement against them because their numbers were so small (120,000) and the opposition so powerful. The Japanese American Citizens League, while denouncing the calls for evacuation, said that if the government deemed it necessary, the Japanese should cooperate to avoid violence.

Their worst fears were realized on March 2, when General DeWitt announced that all Japanese would be removed from the west coast. The orders to evacuate were called Civilian Exclusion

April 1942: A Civilian Exclusion Order posted on a wall in San Francisco.

Family heads
form a line
outside a Civil
Control Center
on Bush Street in
San Francisco
after receiving
their Civilian
Exclusion
Orders.

Orders and were addressed "To All Persons of Japanese Ancestry." These bulletins were posted on walls and telephone poles, printed in newspapers, and announced on the radio. They informed all residents of Japanese descent that they would have to move out of their homes, but no mention was made of where they would be sent. Rather, the orders instructed the head of each family to report to a Civil Control Center, usually a storefront or a school, where the family was assigned a number and told to prepare for departure in one to three weeks. Altogether the military issued 108 Civilian Exclusion Orders in March, April, and May.

With precious little time, the Japanese were driven into a state of panic as the time for their evacuation approached, which became known as E-Day. All along the west coast they conducted hasty evacuation sales. They had no choice. The orders stated that the government was not responsible for any possessions left behind.

A Japanese-owned store in San Francisco's Chinatown conducts an evacuation sale, while next door a Chinese-owned business displays a sign saying "This Is a Chinese Store."

Whites streamed into Japanese neighborhoods and made offers to buy cars, furniture, houses, and farms at ridiculously low prices. Shi remembered them as greedy opportunists. "They swarmed like locusts through the Japanese areas, cheating, stealing, and even threatening people into giving up their belongings for almost nothing."

Driving trucks up and down the streets, the white buyers purchased new washing machines for $5, refrigerators for $10, and sets of living room furniture for $20. After destroying her mother's opera music, Mary Kageyama and her older brother sold the family's beautiful, hand-carved piano for $5. "They came into the neighborhood," Mary said, "and knocked on your door asking to see what you had inside. It was awful."

Before being evacuated, this celery farmer arranged to lease his farm. He holds the lease document in his hand.

With only three days to dispose of their possessions, another Nisei family sold its twenty-six-room hotel for $500. Valued at $6,000, the twenty-two-room Ruth Hotel in Los Angeles was sold for $300. Mary Oda's family sold a new tractor worth $1,200, three cars, three trucks, all their crops, and the thirty acres they farmed in the San Fernando Valley for $1,300. "We couldn't argue," she said. "We had to leave." To avoid the humiliation of giving his property away, one homeowner wanted to burn down his house. "I went to the storage shed to get the gasoline tank and pour the gasoline on my house," he recalled. "But my wife said, 'Don't do it—maybe somebody can use this house. We are civilized people, not savages.'"

But there were many acts of kindness also. White friends

Many farms were taken over by whites after evacuation. A Yugoslav farmer stands outside a berry farm near San Jose, California, that was formerly owned by a Japanese American family.

offered to let their Japanese neighbors store goods and promised to care for property until they returned—if they returned. As Mary Tsukamoto remembered, "It was such a state of confusion and anger, everyone being so upset at what was happening. We sold our brand-new car for practically nothing. Then some wonderful friends came to ask if they could take care of some things we couldn't store. Mr. Lernard, a high school principal, took my piano, and his daughter took our dining table set, which was a wedding gift. They did that for us."

Amy's family packed their possessions in crates and gave

In Oakland, California, moving trucks are loaded with baggage belonging to Japanese American families.

them to Hattie Woods, their next-door neighbor, who was black. Mrs. Woods had two daughters Amy's age, and all three had grown up together as close friends. Hattie volunteered to store the crates in her basement and rent the family home. But with only five days to prepare for evacuation, Amy's father abandoned his produce truck and left the family car on the street.

Shi's father sold the farm and their house for what he could get, and Ruby McFarland offered to store their furniture and other possessions. The farm equipment was put into a garage and locked. Filipino workers for Shi's father promised to take care of it, but the garage was looted and all the farm equipment stolen—something that happened to most Japanese possessions left behind. Still, that mattered little in March 1942. The main concern was to keep the family together.

Accordingly, early in April, Hachizo Nomura moved his family to Los Angeles to live with Shi's aunt. He had learned that the Japanese would be evacuated to specific camps according to where they lived. Altogether, twenty-two members of the Nomura clan lived in the house for about two weeks. Shi recalled, "I can still see the wall-to-wall bodies. In the evenings the families would sit at the dinner table and discuss the new orders of the day. We were not faced with days of decisions as one would imagine, but days of waiting for notices, accepting them, and following orders. This same scene was being repeated everywhere on the coast."

And then, as Shi described it, "The dreaded second eviction notice was distributed to families in our district. Our orders were to pack clothing and toilet articles for each member of the family. Imagine, not a mention of chopsticks and soy sauce among the everyday items!

San Pedro, California: Japanese American families are evacuated by truck.

"We were to assemble at a church in Los Angeles, where we would be loaded on buses and shuttled to the train yard for the trip to Manzanar, which we had heard was in the middle of a desert in eastern California. A few casual onlookers peered over the overpass railing to catch a glimpse of our 'grand exit' from their city, but there were no flowers or speeches. We left the city as quietly and orderly as we had lived.

"The train picked up speed, and the sights of the city and its

Centerville, California: Farm families board an evacuation bus.

Los Angeles: Evacuees board a train for the journey to the Manzanar Relocation Center.

Three-year-old Yukiko Okinaga at the Los Angeles railroad station before being evacuated with her family to Manzanar.

familiar skyline faded in the distance. Choked up and misty-eyed, I leaned back into the hard seat of the day coach and closed my eyes for a moment as the reason for me and my family being on the train became painfully evident. I couldn't accept the fact that we were leaving our friends and our homes, labeled as enemies of our country. Since my early youth, I had always thought of myself as the hero, the good guy. And now I was shoved into the role of the bad guy. What had we done to deserve this? What was our crime?"

4 . MANZANAR

SHI'S FAMILY WAS EVACUATED TO MANZANAR on April 25, 1942. Earlier that month, Amy and her family had been sent to an assembly center at the Santa Anita racetrack. Built to confine the Japanese until permanent camps were constructed, the assembly centers were created in just twenty-eight days. Fashioned from fairgrounds, racetracks, and other open areas, they were enclosed by barbed wire and guarded by armed sentries in towers. In April

and May 110,723 Japanese were escorted into the assembly centers, while another 6,393 were sent straight to permanent relocation camps.

With 18,000 men, women, and children, Santa Anita was the largest assembly center. The horses had been removed only four days before the Japanese started to arrive. Families were housed in horse stalls heavy with manure dust. "Fortunately for us," Amy recalled, "we didn't live in a stall. By the time we got there, they were all taken."

A huge warehouse under construction at the Santa Anita Assembly Center. The racetrack is visible in the foreground.

After their baggage and clothes were searched, Amy's family moved into an open barrack, where they slept on mattresses stuffed with straw. The army had used raw lumber in hastily constructing the building. As the boards dried, gaping cracks appeared in the walls and floors. Within three weeks mushrooms were growing through the floor. Every day Amy went to the main gate where the buses unloaded, until she received word that Shi had been sent to Manzanar.

Manzanar was one of ten permanent relocation centers, or

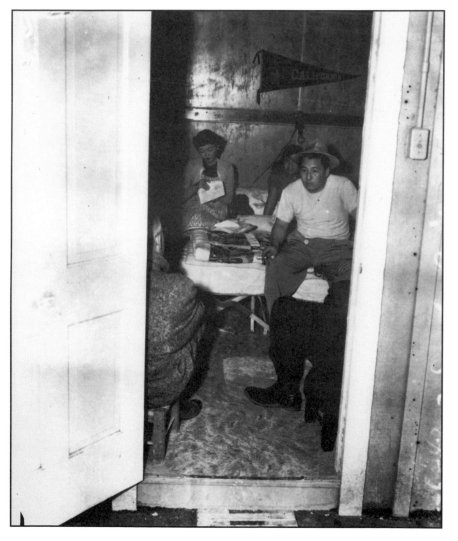

A family of evacuees in their barrack apartment at Santa Anita.

internment camps, built and supervised by the War Relocation Authority. It was located just south of the town of Independence, in Inyo County in eastern California. Two more camps were in Arizona, at Gila River and Poston. Temperatures reached 115 degrees at the latter, and the Japanese poured water on their canvas cots to keep cool in what they jokingly renamed Camp Roastin'. At Minidoka, in Idaho, the average summer temperature was 110 degrees. As Monica Sone recalled, "The sun beat down from above and bounced off the hard-baked earth so that I felt

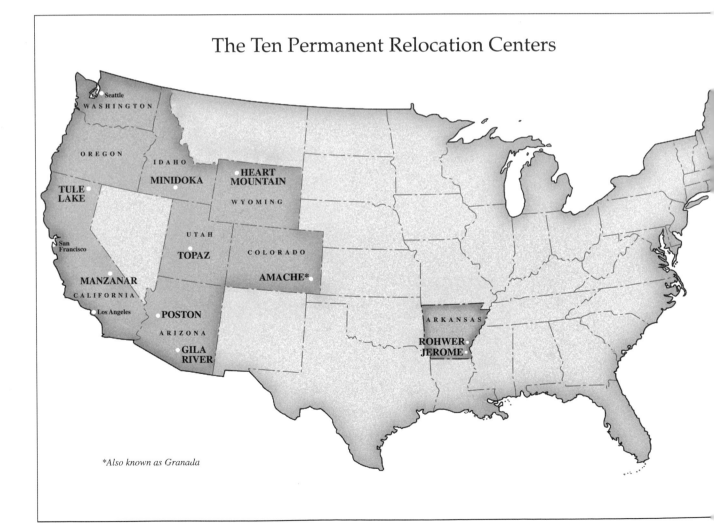

The Ten Permanent Relocation Centers

*Also known as Granada

like a walking southern fried chicken." At Amache, in Colorado, and Heart Mountain, in Wyoming, winter temperatures fell to minus 30 degrees. In November 1942 thirty-two Nisei children were arrested for sneaking out of the Heart Mountain camp and sledding on a nearby hill. At Topaz, in Utah, an elderly Issei was shot and killed in broad daylight for walking too close to the camp's fence. An eight-foot barbed wire fence, a thousand armed soldiers, and six tanks guarded the Japanese interned at the Tule Lake camp in California. The other two camps, Rohwer and Jerome, were in the damp, swampy lowlands of Arkansas, where the most poisonous snakes in North America lived.

Manzanar was modeled after an army base designed to house single men. It was one mile square and divided into thirty-six blocks with twenty-four barracks to a block. Each barrack was 20 feet wide and 120 feet long. Laundry and bathroom facilities were located in the center of each block, each of which had an open mess hall. There was a hospital in one corner of the camp, but the motor pool, warehouses, and administrative offices were located beyond the barbed wire perimeter. At night, searchlights scanned the brush. One of the largest internment camps, Manzanar held over 10,000 men, women, and children guarded by eight towers with machine guns. No area within the camp was beyond the reach of a soldier's bullet.

When Shi arrived at Manzanar, he was greeted by "a great ball of dirty fog." Because of the dust storm, created by the fierce Manzanar wind, Shi did not see the guard towers with their mounted machine guns or the barbed wire fence until the next day. Visibility was near zero, he recalled. "The strong wind picked up rice-sized sand from the construction areas and pelted the buses like buckshot."

Construction of barrack apartments at Manzanar in the spring of 1942.

The buses rolled to a stop in the middle of a firebreak between Blocks 14 and 15. As the twenty-two members of the Nomura family exited, Shi was surprised to see that some of the Japanese had already arrived. Despite the blasting wind, they had come to see if their friends or relatives were aboard. Happily enough, his first experience at Manzanar was humorous. "They were bundled up," he said, "in a comical array of World War I surplus uniforms issued by the War Relocation Authority. They had baggy pants, hanging jackets, wraparound leggings, helmets, goggles—the whole works. They looked like a bunch of refugees from another world!"

Soldiers marched the new arrivals to a mess hall, where their numbers were recorded. Guards searched them, seizing anything they considered dangerous—kitchen knives, knitting needles, even hot plates for warming babies' milk. Each internee was issued a cot, an army blanket, and a sack to be filled with straw for a mattress; then families were assigned to a barrack according to size and number of children. Childless couples had to live in an open barrack, with only sheets hung up as partitions to separate them from strangers. "For these unfortunate people," Shi said, "this was very embarrassing and degrading."

Manzanar as it looked in the early months of occupation: unfinished barracks, piles of building supplies, and wind-blown dust.

The Nomuras were assigned to three apartments in different barracks of Block 21. The apartments had no closets, cupboards, or furniture. In an apartment at the end of one barrack, fifty yards from the barbed wire fence, Shi lived with his mother and father, brother Shigeru and his family, and sister Sadae with her children; her husband, who was Nisei, had joined the army before the bombing of Pearl Harbor and remained stationed on the east coast. This happened to other Nisei families as well; the soldiers were kept away from the west coast while their wives and children were interned there.

The ten people assigned to the twelve-by-twenty-foot room soon made their living quarters as comfortable as possible. By piping water in from an outside faucet, Shigeru and Shi made their mother a little kitchen complete with a small sink and cupboards. They also made stools, benches, and cabinets from scrap lumber and apple crates. In stiff competition with others, Shi collected perhaps fifty lids from tin cans. They were highly valued by all the Japanese families, who nailed them over knotholes in the floor and walls to repel the winds of Manzanar.

Shi awoke on his first morning in Manzanar shivering from the cold. Sitting on the edge of the cot, he surveyed the room that was to be his home for an unknown period. The canvas mattress stuffed with straw was a far cry from the comfort he had once known. Then he had to go to the bathroom. The 250 people living in a block shared common bathroom facilities. On a concrete slab down the center of the room, toilet bowls were arranged in pairs, back to back, with no partitions. As one resident said, "You could hold hands sitting on the pot," and for Shi it was one of the worst things about Japanese internment. "There was no privacy at all. Everyone could see you and you lost your identity as a person because you couldn't even do this alone. We were not like animals going to the bathroom in the woods next to one another, but we were being treated like animals."

Only a few days later he received the news that Amy's family had been sent to Santa Anita. He wrote to her hoping that they would soon be together, and she sent him a green wool sweater with a note. "Finally finished your sweater. I hope it fits. Wear it to keep you warm until we're together. Love, Amy." They wrote

April 1942: Mealtime in one of the newly built mess halls at Manzanar.

to each other almost daily, although some of their letters and packages were "lost" by the police while inspecting the contents. Then, on one of her trips to Manzanar, Ruby McFarland told Shi in a measured voice that Amy had been transferred to Camp Amache in Colorado.

Shi applied for a transfer to the Colorado camp, but there was little chance that it would be approved. He and Amy continued to write to each other, and Ruby visited the camp bringing ration books and news of how the Japanese farms had deteriorated. Many had been taken over by inexperienced whites, who soon concluded that farming was too much work and abandoned the fields. In the meantime, Shi settled into the routine of camp life and decided to look for a job.

Since no family got more than $7.50 per month as an allowance, the men took jobs to buy clothes and other items not provided by the War Relocation Authority; nearly all of the

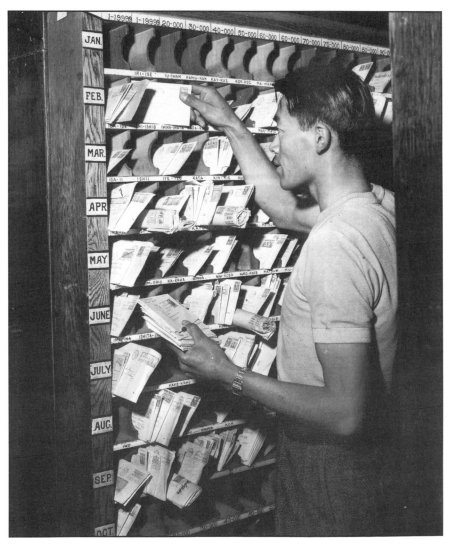

With more than 10,000 residents, Manzanar was like a small town. Services were staffed by internees and included a post office (**opposite**), schools (**top**), and a farm (**bottom**).

women stayed in the barracks to baby-sit. The relocation camps were like small towns. There was much to do in running the schools, health clinics, and mess halls and in staffing other basic services. Agricultural work was available on Manzanar's extensive farm, and a factory had opened to make camouflage nets for the army.

Some Nisei chose not to work because the pay for a forty-hour-a-week job was so low: $8 a month for unskilled labor, $12 for skilled labor, and $16 for professionals such as doctors and dentists. Those who did work were careful to pick jobs with additional benefits. Shi's closest friend in camp, Kow Maruki, took a job driving the mail truck, so that he could visit all the mess halls and eat well. At Amache, Amy took a job as a clerk for the meat department. As a bonus she got to ride the meat truck into the nearby town of Lamar, go shopping, and even see a movie.

In late May, Shi hired on as a timekeeper for the boiler workers who tended the camp's hot water system. He made two rounds of the camp, one in the morning and one in the afternoon. During the morning run, if the weather was nice and people were outside, he made many friends. "I would try to write to my Amy in Camp Amache every night," he recalled, "but I never realized there were so many cute girls around, which made my work more enjoyable."

At night Shi, Kow, and their friends sat around an old oil-burning stove in his apartment and exchanged stories about their high school days. They toasted bread and boiled water in a one-gallon tin can for the cocoa powder they had begged off the chef. Later that summer the War Relocation Authority granted permission to Shi's friend Henry Ushijima to have his record-

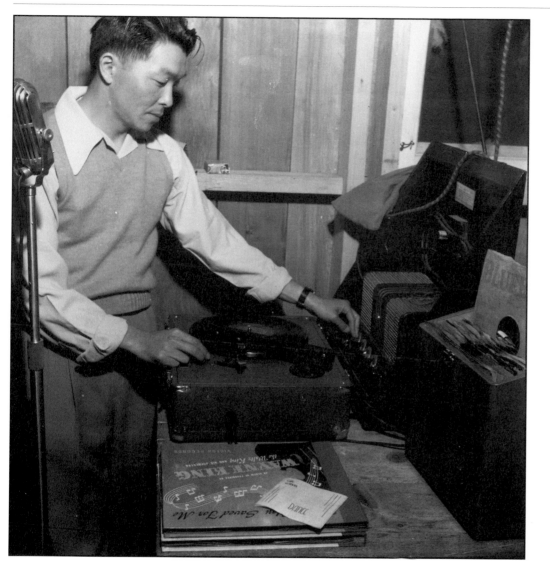

playing equipment shipped to the camp. The group set up Henry's powerful loudspeakers and, with his collection of hit records, transformed the firebreak between Blocks 22 and 23 into an outdoor theater. Shi remembered, "It was especially welcomed by young couples who had no privacy in their apartments. It was common to see couples huddled together in the sand, with an old army blanket draped over their shoulders, enjoying the music and the privacy."

Shi's friend Henry Ushijima with his record-playing equipment. Before being evacuated to Manzanar, Henry was a sound engineer in Hollywood.

But Manzanar was an internment camp, and it was never possible to escape that fact. In July an internee was gathering scrap lumber in an area still under construction, when he was shot by a guard. He was an old man, an Issei, and did not

Workers at Manzanar making camouflage nets for the army. Chemicals in the dye caused skin rashes, and in August 1942, the workers threatened to strike.

understand the order to halt. In August camouflage workers threatened to strike because the chemicals used for dyeing burlap caused them to break out in rashes and sent them to the hospital in droves. The strike was stopped by the military police, who threatened force. And every time Shi received a letter from Amy that had already been opened and read, he was reminded of where he was.

To protest his confinement and gain some solitude, Shi regularly sneaked out of camp. Always at night and usually alone, he slipped through the fence near his apartment and climbed a hill to view the lights of the town of Independence. "The sky was a solid blanket of stars," he remembered. "Mercifully, the guard towers and barbed wire fence would gradually disappear from sight, but the searchlights were an everlasting reminder of the sentries on duty. Many a night I

Left: Amy on visit from Camp Amache to the town of Lamar.
Right: *Shi at Manzanar.*

would climb the hill and look up at a particularly bright star and wonder if Amy was watching the same star in Camp Amache."

After four months of confinement, the government unexpectedly offered Shi an opportunity to leave Manzanar and possibly see Amy. In August 1942 the Department of Labor issued an urgent request for agricultural workers in Colorado, Idaho,

Utah, and Montana. Crops were about to rot there because most eligible men had reported for military duty or had left for high-paying work in defense plants. Although labeled the enemy only months before, the Nisei were asked to show their patriotism by saving the harvest. Afterward the government would grant them certain favors—perhaps transfers to other camps.

Altogether, 10,000 Nisei from various camps enrolled in the sixty-day program. "If it had not been for Japanese labor," one Utah newspaper said, "much of the best crops in the western United States would have been lost." Only California refused to accept the Japanese, importing 30,000 Mexican workers instead.

Manzanar sent approximately 900 Nisei workers, including Shi's crew of four, to the western states. Shi recalled, "Even though the contract only called for sixty days, we could rightfully walk the streets as free citizens and try to regain the dignity we had lost. I might get to Colorado, and we would be leaving the barbed wire fences far behind."

5 . TJADEN'S

SHI'S CREW BOARDED A TRAIN headed for Great Falls, in northern Montana. The train pulled in at nightfall flanked by dozens of farmers who had been arriving since midafternoon. "They were burly men in heavy winter jackets," Shi remembered, "and as our car was uncoupled they approached cautiously to look us over. Most of them were looking at a Japanese face for the first time, and their expressions showed that they had expected to see a bunch of bucktoothed grinning faces wearing horn-rimmed glasses, as we were made out to be in the magazines and movies

A wartime poster presents an image of the Japanese familiar to many Americans: horn-rimmed glasses, narrow, slitted eyes, and a bucktoothed grin.

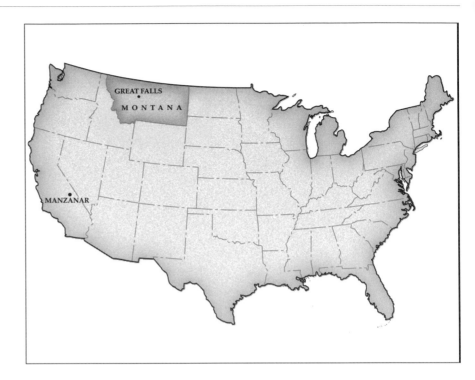

they had seen. We must have really freaked them out when we opened the car windows to exchange greetings. They seemed surprised at our command of the English language."

The farmer assigned to Shi's crew had already hired another crew for an emergency harvest. But many nonregistered farmers were patiently waiting for workers, leaving the Nisei in the enviable position of sizing them up and choosing whom to work for. After a brief period Shi's crew signed with A. T. Tjaden. "We sat and talked awhile with Mr. Tjaden before signing with him," Shi said, "and I think we were swayed by his youthful appearance and thinking. He seemed to be fully aware of our situation and in full sympathy with our cause."

The crew climbed into Tjaden's pickup truck for the sixty-mile drive to Conrad, a small town midway between Great Falls and the Canadian border. Before he left Manzanar, Shi had used his pocket dictionary to look up "furlough," the term authorities used to refer to the leave policy. It meant vacation, but as Shi found out, "This was a far cry from a vacation." While other Nisei were busy saving peas, potatoes, and other crops in warmer climates, Shi's crew was headed to the frozen fields of northern Montana to work one of the hardest crops of all, sugar beets.

Tjaden was slowly paying off his fifty-acre farm with marginal profits from grain and sugar beets. Without Nisei help he would be forced to leave most of his crop in the ground or feed it to his fifty head of cattle, missing his mortgage payment and perhaps losing his farm. Tjaden did not know, and Shi did not tell him, that three of the four crew members had no experience in farming, let alone in cutting sugar beets. Cousin Carl, Shi recalled, "was great with girls but not much for farming." "Lucky" Yamamoto was the son of a pharmacist, and Yoji Ozaki was a student.

When he was awakened the next dawn by a rooster's crow,

Shi's cousin Carl and "Lucky" Yamamoto at the door of the crew's shack at Tjaden's farm.

Shi beet topping in Montana.

Shi was stiff from having slept curled on a cold floor, his leg aching from a nasty crack on the shin he got the night before. There was no running water in the shack where the crew slept, so Shi fetched some in a bucket from the cistern near Tjaden's house. Noticing that he was up, Mrs. Tjaden brought over some bacon and eggs, a jug of fresh milk, and two loaves of bread fresh out of the oven. "This beautiful gesture," Shi said, "was truly a blessing. It was nice to have someone treat us well."

With little time to waste, Tjaden led the crew to a patch of beets, plowed up for a quick lesson in topping. To top the beets he used a large machete with a two-inch barb, or hook, welded on the end. He showed the workers how to pull up a sugar beet with the barb, hold it in one hand, top it with the machete, and toss it aside without lost motion. The crew joined in enthusiastically, but weeks would pass before any of them perfected the technique. "The very first beet I attacked," Shi remembered, "was a huge one and buried deep. It wouldn't yield to my pull. So with my left hand pulling on the beet top, and the barb hooked into the beet, I gave a mighty yank. The barb ripped through the beet—and ripped open the back of my left hand, cutting open a vein. Another bloody mess!"

The first full day of beet topping was typical of the next six weeks. The crew tried to develop a rhythm to make their moves smoother and less tiring, but after an hour of topping Carl and Lucky dropped their machetes, sprawled out on the cold ground, and refused to go any further. Stubbornly, Yoji and Shi kept up the pace and worked until the sun sank to the horizon. They spent the last hour of daylight loading the beets into Tjaden's wagon for the trip to the mill.

Recalling their first day's work Shi said, "We must have been a sorry sight as we dragged ourselves back to our shack. It was painful trying to straighten up after being bent over so long, and I had blisters the size of marbles on my right hand. My left hand was bandaged from the knife wound, and I was limping badly on my right leg from the crack on the shin. It took us a good week to get broken in—which doesn't mean the work got any easier. It just became a little easier to take."

For all of their work in Montana, the internees earned less than $2.00 a day. "But we were free," Shi said, "and that was worth more than any amount of money." Freedom meant having Saturdays off when Tjaden made his weekly trip into Conrad for supplies. Freedom meant hitching a ride in his pickup to go shopping or just walking the streets without soldiers or barbed wire.

On his first trip into Conrad, Shi was surprised that the town was much larger than he expected and bustling with activity. Having heard that a Japanese workforce had arrived in the county, the town's residents turned out to catch a glimpse—many for the first time—of an Asian. "All this attention made us feel uncomfortable," Shi recalled. "There was always the feeling that some of the people we met still looked upon us as enemies, and we were subjected to stares wherever we went. I saw a sign on a barber shop window that read 'Welcome Japs! Ears Lowered FREE!' But I wasn't certain if it meant we could get a free haircut because it referred to us as Japs.

"We rushed through our shopping and loaded the groceries in the pickup, then went across the street to the Pondera Drug Store to get some medical supplies for me and to have that soda I had often dreamed about. At long last the 'drought' was about to end."

Two rough men wearing cowboy hats sat at a table, their eyes following Shi's crew. The Nisei sat at the ice-cream counter, not knowing if they would be served. After what seemed like ages but was only a few minutes, a waitress walked over and—in a surprisingly friendly manner—took the crew's order. With a sigh of relief, Shi ordered a double chocolate soda, his first since entering Manzanar, and he relished it to the last muffled gurgle. Before heading back to the pickup, Shi struck up a conversation with the young, blond waitress, telling her he would see her next week. "Thanks to the friend that I had made in the Pondera Drug Store," he said, "this was our headquarters and the highlight of our weekly trips into Conrad."

The following Saturday he talked to the girl for nearly three hours, but he did not dare ask her out for fear of the town's reaction and because of how he felt about himself after living in Manzanar. "It felt good to be able to walk the streets again as a 'free citizen,'" he remembered. "But somehow it lacked the complete feeling of true freedom. Restriction behind a barbed wire fence had instilled in us a hidden fear. We had freedom of movement, but we knew inside that we were not truly free."

That feeling was reinforced when Shi's crew decided to go to the town's only movie house. "We were coldly escorted up to

the balcony," he recalled. "Later we learned that the section downstairs was reserved for whites only. They put us in the balcony reserved for Indians, and even the Indians refused to sit near us."

The Nisei working on farms near big cities faced less discrimination and could frequent bowling alleys, movie theaters,

Furlough workers at an onion farm near Pueblo, Colorado, in October 1942.

and good restaurants. But those near smaller towns encountered areas "off limits" to Japanese. It was understood that one of these areas was Conrad's only roller-skating rink, the hangout for young people for miles around. On his fourth Saturday in Conrad, Shi was asked by his friend at Pondera's to go on a date, roller-skating.

"The thought occurred to me that I might get into a fight," Shi remembered, "and other such thoughts crossed my mind. But I accepted, hesitantly, because I liked her. Fearing the worst, I opened the door to the rink and she grabbed my arm as we entered. There was a stunned silence as all eyes turned to us. But when she smiled and waved to her friends the room gradually came back to life. My uneasiness was soon overcome by their friendliness and sincerity. From that time on, we got along famously with the young people of Conrad. All it took was to get to know each other."

Two weeks later a mountain of snow fell on the farms of Montana, and Shi's furlough as a beet topper and steady patron of Pondera's came to a close. The fields that he had worked disappeared in one night. At the first sign of the snow, the crew worked twenty-four hours nonstop, but the last of Tjaden's crop was ruined. "After all the sweat, working around the clock, it was a heartbreak ending for all of us," Shi said. Yet Tjaden's farm was saved.

With the onset of winter the crew prepared to leave, but snowdrifts blocked the highway to Great Falls. Shi thought it might not be so bad to be stranded in Conrad for the winter. Furlough workers could remain on the job if they could find permanent employment, and Mr. Tjaden had made Shi the offer. He had noticed that Shi's friendship with the girl at Pondera's had deepened, and he hoped this would influence Shi's decision. "I had given the matter considerable thought," Shi said, "and my heart urged me to stay. But I had come to Montana as a way of transferring to Amache, to see Amy and find out if we still had a future together."

He spent his last day in Conrad shopping and saying good-bye. He remembered, "I was deeply moved by the sincerity of those I had met and it was difficult to keep a dry eye. My crew joined me at the Pondera Drug to say good-bye to the employees and the owner, who was very suspicious of us when we first appeared on the scene six weeks ago. As a parting gesture he treated us to a final round of sodas. It was very difficult to say good-bye to the girl in the drugstore, and I told her that if things didn't work out in Amache I was coming back to Montana. It was on this word that we parted.

"We headed down the street for the last time, past the sign 'Welcome Japs! Ears Lowered Free!' It was still there, slightly soiled and torn at the edges—but crying out to remind us that all was not well. We were still Japs."

6 . SORTING OUT

IN LATE OCTOBER 1942 soldiers carrying rifles with bayonets marched Shi into Manzanar for a second time. Inspectors seized his stash of candy, cookies, and a five-pound bag of sugar that was a gift from Mrs. Tjaden. All were legal items but were highly desired by the guards.

Shi anxiously hurried to his wartime home in Block 21. Although back behind barbed wire he was overcome with a warm feeling of comfort when he was reunited with his family. He got his timekeeper's job back, but he discovered that Manzanar had changed considerably in the last two months—as had the entire story of Japanese internment.

Within weeks after the Japanese were sent to the camps, pressure was brought to obtain the release of some internees. Educators and church leaders were concerned that the younger Nisei were being denied access to higher education. Through their efforts, 250 Nisei were allowed to leave camp by the summer of 1942, to attend universities outside of Restricted Area Number One. Before the end of the year, 4,300 young Nisei had been granted temporary releases for schools in the East and Midwest, although some universities flatly refused to accept any Japanese.

At the same time, the army's intelligence service began recruiting Nisei who could speak Japanese to serve as interpreters. Military officials were astonished to discover how few Nisei actually spoke or understood Japanese. Only a tenth of the first 5,000 interviewed knew enough Japanese to be accepted into service. Ironically, they were sent to a special school in Minnesota to learn the language and customs of Japan, while their own government considered them not American but Japanese—and therefore dangerous.

Altogether, 3,700 Nisei who graduated from the special school served with distinction in the Pacific. The Nisei became one of America's "secret weapons" and their efforts helped save countless American lives, especially in the Philippines. The Nisei translated captured documents and when American soldiers invaded those islands, they knew the complete plans of the Japanese Army.

Nisei soldiers in combat in northern Burma with the 5307th Infantry Regiment, known as Merrill's Marauders.

The Nisei interpreters also joined infantry patrols as scouts and fought in hand-to-hand combat. In Burma and China they fought with the 5307th Infantry Regiment, known as Merrill's Marauders after its commander, Brigadier General Frank D. Merrill. The Nisei crept to enemy lines to listen to what was being said by Japanese soldiers and perhaps learn of an impending attack. They often got caught, and one earned the nickname Horizontal Hank for the many times he was pinned down by gunfire. One of Hank's white comrades wrote home, "Many of the boys, and myself especially, never knew a Japanese American or what one was like. Now we know and the Marauders want you to know that we are backing the Nisei 100 percent. It makes the boys and myself raging mad to read about movements against the Japanese Americans back home. We would dare them to say things like they have in front of us."

Meanwhile, the need for manpower led the military to rethink its policy of excluding the Nisei from the army. At the time of Pearl Harbor about 5,000 Nisei were already in the army, but after that date they were barred from military service, except in the all-Nisei 100th Infantry Battalion of Hawaii. After the Selective Service officially barred the Nisei from enlisting, in September 1942, the Japanese American Citizens League passed a resolution asking that they "be accorded the same privilege of serving our country in the armed forces as that granted to every other American citizen." Because of the success of the furlough program and the need for more fighting men, the War Department dropped the ban in November 1942, announcing that a second all-Nisei combat team would be formed.

In November and December recruiters flocked to the internment camps and offered the Nisei a chance to demonstrate their loyalty by joining the army. Those who did were formed into the 442nd Regimental Combat Team, which saw action in North Africa, France, and Italy along with the 100th Infantry. The motto of the 442nd was "Go for Broke," which meant to fight fanatically—like wild men gone crazy—to defeat the enemy.

And they did fight like fanatics. With 9,486 dead and wounded, the 442nd suffered the highest casualty rate for any American regiment in World War II. It became the most decorated American unit in the war, receiving seven Presidential Unit Citations, 52 Distinguished Service Crosses, and 560 Silver Stars. The men of the 100th earned seventy-four decorations and over 1,000 Purple Hearts, the medal given to those wounded in battle.

The turning point in the war with Japan occurred in June 1942,

Members of the 442nd Regiment— the most decorated American unit to serve in World War II— returning from Europe aboard a troopship in 1945.

with the Japanese defeat at the Battle of Midway, which effectively ended the threat of a Japanese invasion of the western United States coast. It was becoming increasingly difficult to justify Japanese internment on the grounds of military necessity, especially after the Nisei had demonstrated their loyalty by saving crops and volunteering for language school. Accordingly, in the winter of 1942–1943, the War Relocation Authority adopted a program that allowed the Nisei to leave the camps and resettle in forty-two cities in midwestern and eastern states. But the plan was not well thought out, and it created anger and turmoil. In

A sign on a bulletin board at Manzanar announces the leave program.

some camps Nisei rioted over the policy and were shot by soldiers.

The policy was called "sorting out"—separating loyal from disloyal Japanese—and the conflict arose over the loyalty oath that was part of the program. The Japanese were given a questionnaire called an Application for Leave Clearance. At the heart of it lay questions 27 and 28, which required a simple yes or no answer. Question 27 read, "Are you willing to serve in the armed forces of the United States, in combat duty, wherever ordered?" Question 28 read, "Will you swear unqualified allegiance to the United States of America and . . . forswear any form of allegiance or obedience to the Japanese emperor, or any other foreign government, power, or organization?" Answering yes to both questions was essential for army service or clearance to leave the camps. A no answer to either question branded a person as disloyal and ineligible to leave.

At first, many Issei refused to answer the questionnaire. They had lost houses, farms, and most of their possessions and were forbidden to return to their homes, even if they answered yes. But when administrators ordered everyone to answer the questionnaire, the Issei became confused and resentful. If they answered no they would be considered dangerous and, it was rumored, sent to Japan or to harsh confinement at the Tule Lake camp. A yes answer meant renouncing their Japanese citizenship, and since they were prohibited from becoming United States citizens, they would be a people without a country.

The questionnaire tore apart families and set Issei against Nisei, for the Nisei were being asked to choose between their country and their parents. More important, as American citizens who had broken no laws and who had demonstrated their loyalty,

*February 1943:
A U.S. Army
lieutenant explains
the process of
registration for the
draft to a group of
men at Manzanar.*

the Nisei angrily resented having to take an extra pledge of allegiance—especially after their rights as citizens had been unfairly taken away. They had learned American principles of citizenship rights, and by denouncing the insulting loyalty oath they affirmed these principles. One young Nisei answered yes-yes and then asked the supervising officer, "May I go to Phoenix?" When the officer said that Phoenix was a banned area, the young man tore up the questionnaire saying, "That's the way I feel about your attitude toward our citizenship."

Shi answered yes-yes, as did all members of the Nomura family—but not without resentment and anger. He remembered, "Crash meetings were held in every block and they invariably ended in arguments and occasionally fistfights. We had been deprived of our rights. And now we were being asked to prove our worth as citizens, to prove our loyalty to a country that had turned its back on us. What of the other citizens on the other side of the barbed wire fences? What determined their loyalty? What determined their rights to citizenship? Why are they left secure in their homes while we have our privacy invaded?"

In the end, the questionnaire proved meaningless as a test of loyalty: people answered yes or no depending on what they thought would be the result for their family. Before "sorting out" ended in February 1943, question 28 was changed for the Issei to one that asked them to pledge obedience only to the laws of the United States; this made it easy for many to sign. Out of 75,000 adults who answered the questionnaire, only about 8,500 answered no-no. Government officials were surprised that more Nisei than Issei were no-no's. But rather than being disloyal, these Nisei were standing up for their rights as citizens. The Tule Lake camp was cleared and all no-no's were sent there, including 5,700 Nisei—American citizens who had renounced their citizenship because they had been imprisoned without trial or even a charge of wrongdoing.

As the government's attitude toward the Japanese changed, it became clear to some officials that internment might have been a mistake. After "sorting out" ended, all young Nisei who answered yes-yes were subject to the draft. But before they could be drafted, most of them volunteered for service. Most of the yes-yes males of suitable age eventually served in the army, a surprisingly large number, 33,000. Along with the Nisei interpreters and furlough workers, this also helped expose the lies used to justify Japanese internment. When President Roosevelt

The outstanding military service of Nisei soldiers helped change attitudes toward Japanese Americans as the war went on. Under Secretary of War Robert P. Patterson congratulates a member of the "Go for Broke" 442nd Regiment.

approved the plan to organize an all-Nisei combat unit on February 1, 1943, he declared, "No loyal citizen of the United States should be denied the democratic right to exercise the rights of citizenship, regardless of ancestry. . . . Americanism is not, and never was, a matter of race or ancestry." Milton Eisenhower, director of the War Relocation Authority, said, "I feel most deeply that when the war is over we as Americans are going to regret the avoidable injustices that have been done."

However, there was little change in the public's attitude toward the Japanese. The popular Humphrey Bogart film *Across*

the Pacific portrayed a Nisei all-American type as a spy plotting to bomb the Panama Canal. California's former attorney general Earl Warren, now the state's governor, told a meeting of governors in June 1943 that the Japanese should not be released, because "No one will be able to tell a saboteur from any other Jap." California was still closed to the Japanese, and uniformed Nisei servicemen passing through Los Angeles to visit their parents in Manzanar still saw the same signs: "No Japs."

Partly for this reason, only about 36,000 Issei and Nisei participated in the leave program, including Shi, whose FBI clearance was granted on May 14, 1943. "Now what was I going to do?" he wondered. "Go back to Montana? Fulfill my promises in Amache? Or stay with my family and friends in Manzanar?

"I had been drafted, but my medical records from the shot-put accident made me ineligible to serve. When I notified Amy of my clearance, she immediately requested permission for my admission to Amache. But so much had happened in the thirteen months since we had been separated. I was not really sure of her true feelings or mine. How could we live as husband and wife in a concentration camp? I felt it would never work out. But seeing other people leaving Manzanar to be reunited with loved ones made me realize that my first duty was to Amy."

7 . THE SONGBIRD OF MANZANAR

SHI LEFT FOR COLORADO in June 1943 with the intention of marrying Amy. He carried a diamond engagement ring purchased with his savings and a loan from his father. Traveling by train to the town of Lamar and then by bus, Shi entered the Amache camp, where the guards failed to look in his mouth and find the ring.

He tried to renew his relationship with Amy, but as the days passed it became clear that she had other boyfriends. After three months he confronted her and there were two versions of what happened. Said Shi: "I told her I loved her and I proposed marriage, but she was having too much fun playing the field and she said no. With tears in my eyes, I threw the ring in the desert and told her good-bye."

"The timing was all wrong," Amy said. "We didn't know what was going to happen to our lives. I really felt bad, and I'm sorry I hurt him, but the timing was all wrong." And so it ended in one afternoon; nearly twenty years would pass before Shi saw Amy again.

Heartbroken, but relieved that this nagging question had been settled at last, Shi reenlisted in the furlough program—only to learn that there was no call for workers in Montana. Instead, he went to Denver and worked in an icehouse, loading blocks of ice onto railroad cars for shipping vegetables east. He earned nearly $50 in two months, but the labor was hard and humiliating. "People at the train station would stop and stare, just as they did along Highway 395 at the front gate in Manzanar," he recalled of this bleak period. "They would get out of their cars and stare at the Japanese crew and whisper who knows what."

Shi returned to Manzanar in August 1943 and worked as sportswriter for the *Manzanar Free Press*, the camp's newspaper, and also for Dr. Robert Emerson on the experimental rubber farm he built at Manzanar. World War II had cut off America's main source of rubber, from Malaya. Dr. Emerson and chemist Shinpei Nishimura conducted experiments until they perfected a method for producing high-quality rubber that was superior to Malayan rubber. Dr. Emerson became Shi's close friend. "He firmly believed in the loyalty of the Japanese," Shi said, "and he made us feel proud of our contribution to fighting the enemy."

Shi's final months in Manzanar were dominated by sports, as

Dr. Robert Emerson (right) demonstrates part of the process he developed for producing rubber to members of the nursery staff at Manzanar.

his life had been in high school. The firebreaks between Blocks 14 and 15 were leveled, and a softball diamond and football field were built—although the players faced a constant battle with the wind, which would create sudden dust storms, ending the afternoon games. Hundreds showed up for the games, but more could be expected—as well as a chorus of boos—whenever a team called the Yogores took the field. Tough youths from the Los Angeles fishing communities of Terminal Island and San Pedro, the Yogores went barefoot, bullied people who got in their way, and accused others of not being Japanese enough. Whether by

One of Munzanar's baseball diamonds in use.

design or by accident, Shi's football team had beaten the Yogores and the Yogores wanted revenge. Thousands attended the return match. The end result was twofold: Shi's team won the game but lost the post-game fight.

It was around this time, December 1943, that Shi was out walking with friends when he heard a voice echoing from a mess hall where a dance was being held. "When we neared the hall, which was beautifully decorated with twisted strips of colorful crepe paper, a lovely voice could be heard coming over the public address system. As the voice drifted over to me in the still air, it struck a forgotten chord deep in my memories, taking me back to August 1941."

The voice was the one that had held Shi spellbound two years earlier at Yamato Hall. It belonged to Mary Kageyama, who had been sent to Manzanar from Los Angeles. Her father had died when she was two years old. Her mother taught Japanese singing, dancing, and musical instruments, gave voice lessons to white students studying American music; and taught her seven-year-old daughter how to sing the popular songs of the day.

Mary was only seven when her mother died in 1933. Mary's older brother Frank and older sister Fumi, who were sixteen and fifteen at the time, dropped out of school to save Mary and her two younger sisters from the orphanage. Through books in the public library, Frank learned horticulture and with Fumi established a gardening business that kept the family intact.

As a student at Venice High School, Mary was shy, and her closest friends—most of whom were white—shared her interest in music. She sang in the choir, performed in talent shows, and entertained soldiers at army bases. She won first prize at Yamato Hall in 1941.

Mary was sixteen when she helped destroy her mother's opera music and prepare for evacuation. Her brother Frank had just purchased a 1939 Buick, which he took to one of his white customers, who put it on blocks and ran the motor once a week. The family had no idea of where they were being sent; they were told only that the place had rattlesnakes and scorpions. Consequently, they boarded the bus for Manzanar wearing newly purchased cowboy boots.

Mary resumed her studies at one of the camp's high schools set up by the government, graduated in 1943, and went to work as a file clerk for the camp's public works department, which maintained the electricity and plumbing. She continued studying music and joined the Modernaires, a girl's social club that sponsored dances where Mary sang. "Mary was the star," Mas Okui said, "but she would never say so." By 1943 she was known throughout the camp as the Songbird of Manzanar.

By this time, Shi's nightly snack group had grown to thirty and had formed a club, the ManzaKnights, which sponsored an annual Thanksgiving dance. In November 1944, as adviser to the club, Shi asked the Modernaires for two entertainers; Mary was selected, along with a tap dancer. Shi had not forgotten his glimpse of Mary the previous December, and on learning that her boyfriend had just moved to Wisconsin, he arranged to escort her for the evening.

"He was a fast worker," Mary said. "I thought he was very handsome, but I thought he was too fast for me." Much to Shi's delight, she sang "Liebestraum," and in between performances they danced. After the blind date, Mary was surprised when Shi kept asking her out. She was charmed by his persistence—but also a little puzzled, for he never told her about Yamato Hall.

After dating steadily for a month, Mary admitted that she had become "starry-eyed."

They went to socials and outdoor concerts, snuggling under blankets in the cold winter months. For the 1944 New Year's Eve dance the ManzaKnights made *moche*, a rice cake traditional for the Japanese New Year. The dance brought them close together, and others noticed the couple. "The one thing about Manzanar," Mary said, "everyone knew your business. It was impossible to be alone." Not quite—for occasionally when Shi sneaked out of camp he was accompanied by the Songbird of Manzanar.

By February 1945 Shi had proposed marriage, Mary had

Mary Kageyama, the Songbird of Manzanar.

Members of the ManzaKnights making moche, *traditional Japanese New Year's rice cakes, for their 1944 New Year's Eve dance. Shi is holding the lid of the wooden barrel in the foreground; his brother, Shigeru, is pounding the rice cake with a mallet.*

accepted, and with the end of war in sight, the military police had been withdrawn from Manzanar. Shi and Mary agreed not to wed until they were released from camp, when they would have a chance for a more normal life. "We took things day by day," Mary said. "We hated the camp—hated it more and more as the day for our release grew closer. There was only one good thing about it. If it wasn't for Manzanar, I wouldn't have met Shi."

Perhaps. For Shi, destiny had willed they be together. "I knew from the moment I heard her sing at Yamato Hall that I would marry this girl. The bombing of Pearl Harbor, the evacuation, and

the difficult adjustment to camp life had made me forget about her. But as I stood by the mess hall listening, her voice released a flood of memories. There, in the one-mile-square compound at night, I heard the voice and I knew it was meant for me, calling me to her, the Songbird of Manzanar."

8 . I AM AN AMERICAN

Early in 1945 Louis Frizzell, a music teacher in Manzanar, stopped at the nearby Lone Pine Café and ordered bacon and eggs. The waitress barked that there was no bacon; it had all been shipped to Manzanar "to feed the Japs." When a burly truckdriver said that he had just unloaded a shipment of bacon at the camp, other patrons shouted "Damn Japs!" and "Send the Japs home!" Frizzell tried to explain that the bacon was earmarked for white employees, but the customers would hear none of it. When they saw a Japanese American they continued to think "Japanese" and not "American."

But for other Americans, when they saw a Japanese they felt shame. Having learned of the Nisei's magnificent combat record, many concluded that a great injustice had been done to the Japanese. For example, in 1943 Mayor Fletcher Bowron had said he did not want the Japanese to return to Los Angeles and that they should be stripped of their citizenship; in 1945 he held a public ceremony at City Hall to welcome the internees home saying, "We want you and all other citizens of Japanese ancestry here to feel secure in your homes." Justice Department lawyer Tom Clark, who later became a Supreme Court justice, declared, "I've made a lot of mistakes in my life and one is my part in the evacuation of the Japanese. We picked them up and put them in concentration camps. That's the truth of the matter and it was wrong." Even Earl Warren, who had led the charge for internment, later confessed, "Whenever I think of the innocent little children I am conscience-stricken. It was wrong to act so impulsively without evidence of disloyalty."

It was in this atmosphere of acceptance and rejection that Japanese internment ended—happily, painfully, curiously. By 1944 there was no longer any military necessity for internment. Consequently, in the spring of 1944 the War Department recommended to President Roosevelt that the confinement of the Japanese be ended. The President agreed and on December 17, 1944, rescinded General DeWitt's mass exclusion order. In January 1945 the War Relocation Authority quietly announced that the camps would be closed by the end of the year. And so, with little fanfare, almost silently in the middle of the night as a thief sneaks away, Japanese internment ended, without a thank-you to the furlough workers, without an apology or a gesture of regret, without compensation for lost homes, jobs, and businesses. The Japanese still in camps were released to face, once again, a hostile white population.

News of what had happened to the "scouts," the first to resettle, sent a chill through the camps and soured the anticipation of freedom. To prevent the return of the Japanese, some whites formed organizations such as No Japs Incorporated in San Diego and the Home Front Commandoes in Sacramento. Early in 1945, in Placer County, California, shots were fired at Nisei farmhouses from speeding cars, barns and fields suddenly caught fire, and Nisei received anonymous telephone threats. In Hood River, Oregon, the American Legion removed the names of Nisei servicemen from the town's honor roll, and 500 residents signed a newspaper notice telling the Japanese they were not wanted. In some cities Japanese were refused permits to reopen their businesses, while California Congressman Clair Engle ranted, "We don't want the Japs back in California and the more we can get rid of the better."

Of all the accounts of harsh postwar treatment, Senator Daniel Inouye's stood out as perhaps the most painful. After spending two years in a hospital recovering from his combat wounds, Captain Inouye checked out in 1947 and decided to get a haircut before returning home to Hawaii:

> "Are you Chinese?" the man said to me.
>
> I looked past him at the three empty chairs, the other two barbers watching us closely. "I'm an American," I said.
>
> "Are you Chinese?"
>
> "I think what you want to know is where my father was born. My father was born in Japan. I'm an American." Deep in my gut I knew what was coming.
>
> "Don't give me that American stuff," he said swiftly. "You're a Jap and we don't cut Jap hair."
>
> I wanted to hit him. I could see myself—it was as though I was standing in front of a mirror. There I stood, in full uniform, the new captain's bars bright on my shoulder, four rows of ribbons on my chest, the combat infantry badge, the distinguished unit citations—and a hook where my hand was supposed to be. And he didn't cut Jap hair. To think that I had gone through a war to save his skin— and he didn't cut Jap hair.

Once again, whites battled whites over the Japanese, as they had in 1942 during the ten weeks between Pearl Harbor and Executive Order No. 9066. Movie stars and other celebrities endorsed the acceptance of Japanese Americans. Most veterans groups, including the American Legion, honored the bravery of Nisei soldiers, as the achievements of the 442nd Regimental

Combat Team helped many white Americans overcome their anti-Japanese prejudices. A hero of the Pacific war, General Joseph Stillwell, came to California to award the Distinguished Service Cross to the family of a Nisei who had died in combat. When he heard that the family had been driven from their home by a gang of whites, he exploded, "The Nisei bought an awful big chunk of America with their blood. I say we soldiers ought to form a pickax club to protect Japanese Americans who fought the war with us. Any time we see a barfly commando picking on these kids or discriminating against them, we ought to bang him over the head with a pickax. . . . We cannot allow a single injustice to be done to the Nisei without defeating the purpose for which we fought."

The closing of the camps was a gradual process that started in January 1945 and ended in December. In January 1,000 left the camps, by February the figure had doubled, and by September 15,000 people were moving out each month. From Arkansas to Wyoming to California, families secured transportation from friends on the outside and arranged for temporary housing. Some tried to go home, others went to a hostel or trailer park set up for temporary residence, while still more moved in with relatives who had already been released.

Bracing to enter the outside world, Mary left Manzanar in February 1945 and Shi in March, both escorted by Mary's brother driving his Buick. Shi's friend Dr. Robert Emerson rented an apartment in Pasadena, where Mary's family stayed while Shi found temporary residence in a trailer park nearby. Shi's parents left Manzanar in November and moved back to Los Angeles, starting a shoe repair business in a store leased from a Chinese family. Shortly after Mary's release, Dr. Emerson took her shopping at Barker Brothers. A clerk asked Mary, "You're not one of those dirty Japs, are you?" They both looked at her, put down the items they were about to buy, and walked out of the store.

Like virtually all the internees, Mary's and Shi's families were financially wiped out by the evacuation. A postwar survey revealed that 80 percent of the goods privately stored by the Japanese were rifled, stolen, or sold during internment. The Japanese lost an estimated $400 million in property, not counting land values that had increased during the war. One government study placed the total losses of property and income from 1942 to 1945 at $6.2 billion in current dollars. There was no formula for calculating the pain and shattered dreams.

"It was easy to be resentful," Shi said. "We had lost our possessions and had been confined by barbed wire and guard

Leaving Manzanar by bus.

towers, and we were still viewed by some as the enemy. I remember a woman in Denver and her two children staring at us. They seemed to come closer for a better look, and I felt like some strange new animal they had never seen before. I turned to her and shouted, 'I am an American citizen! Don't you understand?' Everything stopped and she looked at me and nodded, as if she understood. I have often thought about this woman, who didn't know us at all. We didn't know her, but in the brief moment she saw the injustice of our situation. I wonder why there weren't more like her.

Members of the Tacoma Buddhist Temple in Tacoma, Washington, stored their property at the temple before they were evacuated. During their absence, the temple was broken into and their belongings pilfered.

"The last thing I thought about as we turned onto Highway 395 and I looked back at the camp's main gate was that Mary was waiting for me. Tumbleweeds were rolling through the space where the main gate once was and between the fence posts that had once been strung with barbed wire. It was over, but there were no tears as we sped down the highway, far away from the past and hopeful of the future."

EPILOGUE

DURING WORLD WAR II the United States Supreme Court upheld the constitutionality of interning American citizens of Japanese ancestry in what has been called "the darkest hour in the Court's history." In 1980, Congress, pressured by the Japanese American Citizens League, established the Commission on Wartime Relocation and Internment of Civilians to investigate the events that led to Executive Order No. 9066. It concluded that there was no legal or moral basis for Japanese internment and that the evacuation was caused by "race prejudice, war hysteria and a failure of political leadership."

The report recommended a payment of $20,000 to each internee and that the government apologize for the illegal act. Congress accepted the recommendations and the government ultimately paid $38,474,140 in property claims to Japanese Americans. This was less than 10 percent of their value in 1942.

In a series of cases following World War II the courts struck down California's Alien Land Law, and in 1948 voters rejected a new alien land law by a margin of three to two. The Immigration and Nationality Act of 1952 repealed the Immigration Act of 1924 and allowed Issei to become naturalized citizens. In 1987 the

Court finally declared Japanese internment unconstitutional, calling it "one of the worst violations of civil liberties in American history."

In 1947 Amy married Tatsumi Mizutani. Tat had made camouflage nets in Manzanar, topped sugar beets in Montana as a furlough worker, volunteered for Japanese language school, and served as a translator of enemy documents until the end of the war. He met Amy in New York City, where she had gone from

Mary, Shi, and their first child, Alan, 1947.

Amache to live with her married sister. Tat earned a degree in engineering from New York University and worked as an engineer for the Northrop Corporation in Los Angeles for thirty years until he retired in 1986. Having learned Japanese after the war, Amy worked as a bilingual instructor for the Cypress school district and retired in 1986. Still living in Cypress, California, Amy and Tat have five children and five grandchildren.

Shi married Mary in June 1945. He worked as a gardener, then as a furniture salesman and sewing machine salesman. In 1956 he started his own fish market and grocery store, which he ran successfully until he retired in 1981. Shi and Mary have five children and eleven grandchildren. In 1954 Shi's father, Hachizo, became a naturalized citizen. "He studied so hard," Mary recalled. "He knew the width and breadth of the United States, all the members of Congress, and the height of all the mountain ranges." Mary accompanied Hachizo to the naturalization office for testing. "The tester only asked him one question. Pointing at a bust of Abraham Lincoln on his desk he asked, 'Who's that?' When he replied, 'Abe-ah-rah-ham Lin-con,' the man said, 'Right. You pass.'"

In the early 1970s Shi established the Manzanar Room in the Eastern California Museum in Independence to preserve the memory of the camp. His friend Mas Okui also worked on the museum's Manzanar project. Shi and Mary still make an annual visit to the site of the camp and join other former internees in periodic reunion dinner dances, where the featured performer is still the Songbird of Manzanar. Tat, Amy, Shi, and Mary all shared dinner and memories at the 1961 reunion in Los Angeles.

In October 1990 Shi Nomura received a letter of apology from President George Bush that read, in part:

A monetary sum and words alone cannot restore lost years or erase painful memories; neither can they fully convey our Nation's resolve to rectify injustice and to uphold the rights of individuals. We can never fully right the wrongs of the past. But we can take a clear stand for justice and recognize that serious injustices were done to Japanese Americans during World War II.

From his retirement home in Garden Grove, California, Shi said, "One of the greatest things about America is that it admits its mistakes." But he added, "Some people still identify American citizens of Japanese ancestry with the nation of Japan. This is a great mistake and it's un-American. Just recently, when an anti-whaling group wanted to protest Japan's whaling policy, it marched in Los Angeles's Little Tokyo section and picketed the stores there. This would never have taken place in a Polish or Irish neighborhood."

Referring to internment, he said, "It's easy to think that this is just a part of Japanese history. But it's really a part of American history, because this is what America is all about: tolerating different cultures, accepting people who look different. America is a nation of immigrants from all over the world, and they have made America the greatest country in the world. When anyone sees a person of Japanese ancestry living in the United States, they should first think 'American' and only afterward 'Japanese.' That is the American way."

Shi Nomura, 1991.

To Shi and Mary Nomura,
with special thanks to
Amy and Tat Mizutani,
Mas Okui,
and my wife, Dorothy,
who suggested the book
and pressed for five years
until it was written

BIBLIOGRAPHIC NOTE

INFORMATION CONCERNING JAPANESE FARMING and the anti-Japanese movement, the decision to intern the Japanese, the process of relocation, the assembly centers and relocation camps, the furlough program, "sorting out," and the military contribution of the Nisei, were drawn from the following sources:

John Armor and Peter Wright, *Manzanar* (New York: Times Books, 1988); Jacobus ten Broek, Edward N. Barnhart, and Floyd W. Matson, *Prejudice, War and the Constitution: Cases and Consequences of the Evacuation of the Japanese Americans in World War II* (Berkeley: University of California Press, 1954); Stetson Conn, "Japanese Evacuation from the West Coast," in Stetson Conn, Rose C. Engelman, and Byron Fairchild, *Guarding the United States and Its Outposts* (Washington, D.C.: U.S. Government Printing Office, 1964), pp. 115-149; Roger Daniels, *Concentration Camps USA: Japanese Americans and World War II* (New York: Holt, Rinehart & Winston, 1971); Roger Daniels, *The Decision to Relocate the Japanese Americans* (New York: Lippincott, 1975); Daniel S. Davis, *Behind Barbed Wire: The Imprisonment of Japanese Americans During World War II* (New York: Dutton, 1982); Audrie Girdner and Anne Loftis, *The Great Betrayal: The Evacuation of the Japanese-Americans During World War II* (New York: Macmillan, 1969); Morton Grodzins, *Americans Betrayed: Politics and the Japanese Evacuation* (Chicago: University of Chicago Press, 1949); Bill Hosokawa, *Nisei: The Quiet Americans* (New York: Morrow, 1969); Daniel K. Inouye and Lawrence Elliott, *Journey to Washington* (Englewood Cliffs, N.J.: Prentice-Hall, 1967); Peter H. Irons, *Justice at War: The Story of the Japanese American Internment Cases* (New

York: Oxford University Press, 1983); Daisuke Kitagawa, *Issei and Nisei: The Internment Years* (New York: Seabury Press, 1967); Dillon S. Myer, *Uprooted Americans: The Japanese Americans and the War Relocation Authority During World War II* (Tucson: University of Arizona Press, 1971); Edward H. Spicer, *Impounded People: Japanese-Americans in the Relocation Centers* (Tucson: University of Arizona Press, 1969); Jerry Stanley, "Justice Deferred: A Fifty-Year Perspective on Japanese-Internment Historiography," *Southern California Quarterly* (Summer 1992), pp. 181-206; Chester Tanaka, *Go for Broke: A Pictorial History of the Japanese American 100th Infantry Battalion and the 442nd Regimental Combat Team* (Honolulu: Bess Press, 1988); John Tateishi, *And Justice for All: An Oral History of the Japanese American Detention Camps* (New York: Random House, 1984); Michi Weglyn, *Years of Infamy: The Untold Story of America's Concentration Camps* (New York: Morrow, 1976); and Arthur Zich, "Japanese Americans: Home at Last," *National Geographic* (April 1986), pp. 512-539.

Executive Order No. 9066 is reprinted in U.S. Congress, House Select Committee Investigating National Defense Migration, 77th Congress, 2nd Session, 1942, *House Report 2124*; the findings of the Commission on Wartime Relocation and Internment of Civilians are in *Personal Justice Denied* (Washington, D.C.: U.S. Government Printing Office, 1982).

Information relating to Shi and Mary Nomura, Amy and Tat Mizutani, and Mas Okui came from personal interviews with Shi in Garden Grove, California, on September 12, 1986; with Shi, Mary, and Mas in Garden Grove on January 23, 1993; with Amy and Tat in Cypress, California, on April 25, 1993; with Shi and Mary in Garden Grove on June 16, 1993; and from Shi's account of his wartime experiences in the *Inyo County Museum Bulletin,* October 1974–June 1976; extracts were edited for clarity.

Bill Michael, director of the Eastern California Museum of Inyo County, was helpful in locating material about Manzanar; and David

Self provided valuable criticism of the manuscript. Additional research was provided by Joan Marks, librarian at Banning High School; Peggie Gaughan, librarian at the Delano Branch of the Kern County Library; Pamela and Sara Peterson; and Ben Chavez.

PICTURE CREDITS

The War Relocation Authority (WRA) employed photographers to record the events of the internment. The following photographs are taken from the WRA collection and are reprinted by courtesy of the National Archives: pages 3, 9, 14, 15, 19, 24, 27, 28, 29, 30, 31, 32, 35 (*top*), 50, and 73 by Dorothea Lange; pages i, 22, 34, 35 (*bottom*), 36, 38, 39, 42, 45, and 46 by Clem Albers; pages 47 (*top*), 49, and 68 by Francis Stewart; pages 18 and 85 photographer unknown.

Ansel Adams visited and photographed Manzanar at the request of Camp Director Ralph Merritt in the fall of 1943. His photographs appear on pages 37, 47 (*bottom*), 66, 74, and 84, courtesy of the Library of Congress.

Pages 1, 43, and 70 courtesy of the Library of Congress. Page 11 courtesy of Phineas Banning High School, Wilmington, California. Pages 6 and 8 by Visual Communications Archives. Page 53 and 65 by Culver Pictures. Pages 16 and 63 by AP/Wide World Photos. Page 59 by Bettmann Archive.

Pages 5, 12, 51, 77, 88, and 91 from the collection of Shi Nomura, courtesy of the author; pages 55, 56, and 78 from the collection of Shi Nomura, courtesy of the Eastern California Museum.

INDEX

ABOUT THE AUTHOR

JERRY STANLEY WAS BORN IN Highland Park, Michigan, in 1941. When he was seventeen he joined the air force and was stationed in California. While in college, he supported himself as a rock 'n' roll drummer. He received both his master's and doctorate from the University of Arizona. He is now professor of history at California State University at Bakersfield, where he teaches courses on the American West, the American Indian, and California history.

Among Mr. Stanley's hobbies are bowling, racquetball, fishing, drumming, and writing humor. He is the author of numerous articles for both scholarly journals and popular magazines. His first book, *Children of the Dust Bowl: The True Story of the School at Weedpatch Camp* (1992), was named a Notable Book for Children by the American Library Association. Among the awards it received were the Orbis Pictus Award for outstanding nonfiction for children, the California Library Association's John and Patricia Beatty Award, and the Virginia Library Association's Jefferson Cup.

Mr. Stanley and his wife, Dorothy, live in Bakersfield.